Princess Rachel

KATHRYN OWENS

To order additional copies of this book, contact:
Xlibris
844-714-8691
www.Xlibris.com
Orders@Xlibris.com

ISBN: Softcover   978-1-6698-4703-8
             EBook   978-1-6698-4702-1

Print information available on the last page

Rev. date: 09/20/2022

Once upon a time there was a beautiful princess named Rachel. She lived with her father, King Jeremiah, and mother, Queen Elizabeth.

Everyday day Princess Rachel sat at her bedroom window and gazed at the world beyond. It looked so different from their kingdom and she longed to explore it.

But King Jeremiah refused her every request to travel, demanding all her time be devoted to her school work.

"Study, study, study," the princess complained to her stuffed bear 'Teddy Bearable,' "day in and day out it's the same thing! How much education can a person use?! All these books I read can't possibly help me when I get out into the world!

"Oh, how I would love to see something beyond the boundaries of our kingdom!"

The bear stared blankly back at her. "Oh, you're no help!" She set him down on the window seat and climbed up onto the sill. Although she loved her mother and father, and did enjoy her studies, she decided to sneak away.

Squeezing her eyes tightly, she jumped from the high tower into the surrounding moat.

When the Princess landed in the water, the force of her weight caused the spray to form a giant bubble around her. She pounded on the sides of the bubble but could not burst them.

"Oh my! What have I done?!" she gasped. "Can't someone help me?!" She watched helplessly as she floated quickly toward the opening of the moat into the ocean. She screamed as she sank into the darkness of the sea.

Just as the princess made her plea, her teddy bear sprang to life. He leaped to the window ledge and looked at the water below. "I hear you Princess! I'm comin'!" He paused. "Gotta get rid of this ol' bow first! I'm no baby! I'm gonna save the princess!"

He tore the bow from around his neck and leaped into the air, his arms flailing all the way down.

He hit the water with a gigantic splash and swam toward the bubble.

The princess pounded on the sides of it as he neared. "Teddy Bearable! Help me!" she pleaded.

He nodded and swam under the bubble, trying to push it up, but it was too heavy for him.

"You must get help!" the princess cried.

Teddy swam through the ocean screaming for help.

A beautiful gray porpoise swam up to him.

"Princess is sinkin'!" Teddy screamed. "Princess is sinkin'! OH NO! Help us!"

The porpoise hooked its fin under Teddy's arm as he pointed in the direction they needed to go. They sped off.

The porpoise saw the bubble with the princess inside and swam to it. He carefully pushed it toward the light. But when they reached the surface, they saw that they had been pushed up right between two ships in battle! Teddy dunked back under the water and the porpoise swam away.

Princess Rachel waved her arms in the air and yelled for the sailors to stop fighting. The ship on the left did so immediately. The other ship fired off a few more shots.

Teddy popped his head up and said, "Maybe they didn't hear you," then quickly went back under water.

"Or maybe they don't understand!" The princess waved her arms in the air toward the second ship. "Alto!" she cried, "Alto, Porfavor!"

The second ship stopped firing.

She pulled Teddy up to the surface. "Teddy! They're Spanish! They speak another language!"

Princess Rachel called for each ship to come closer. As they did, she could see both captains looking at her through binoculars.

The ships stopped and dropped down their ladders and the captains climbed down them, looking at the princess and the bear curiously.

"Why are you fighting?" she asked each in their own language.

The Spanish captain pointed at Cap'n Tuna.

"Well," Cap'n Tuna stuttered, "we called out to them to join us for lunch and they started ranting in that fast and different way, and we, ah, we got scared!"

"So you shot at them?!" the princess demanded.

Cap'n Tuna turned bright red.

"He is crazy in the head!" Cap'n Trucha exclaimed angrily in his language. He looked closely at the princess. "You are pale, yet you speak like me. How is this so?"

"I learned your language from the instructors where I come from. I also learned in my history class that fighting and war aren't the best way to resolve things! The wisest way to get results is to sit down together, talk over your differences and disagreements, then both sides must compromise - each giving up something to the other - and find a happy middle ground that everyone can live with. There is always a way that we can get along if each side is willing to work with the other!"

She repeated this to Cap'n Tuna in English. He blushed again.

"Excuse me miss," Cap'n Tuna began. "Could you apologize for us? We really don't want to have any conflict with this fellow, he actually seems quite nice!"

"I would be delighted to!" she said. Princess Rachel gave Cap'n Trucha Cap'n Tuna's heartfelt apologies and he gladly accepted.

The two shook hands.

"Now to prevent problems in the future," the princess said to each, "might I suggest that you draw up an agreement, which we call a treaty, with the rules of peace between the two of you. And also teach each other your languages so there won't be any more misunderstandings!"

Both agreed happily and shook hands again.

"I'd like to do something for you since you've been such a great help to us!" Cap'n Tuna said.

"Would you happen to have a map that I could look at?" the princess asked. "You see, at home, my instructors taught me how to find my way around in a class called 'Geography,' and I really am very anxious to go home."

"Why yes indeed!" Cap'n Tuna answered. "Our navigator has quite a few maps! That's also how we find our way!"

"Yea well, maps aside," Teddy Bearable finally said, "didn't I hear you talkin' about some kinda food or something?!"

"Yes you did, Mr. Bear! So would you all like to join me for lunch before you go?" Cap'n Tuna offered.

Everyone agreed and sat down together for a delightful meal, after which the captain showed Princess Rachel to the map room.

"Excuse me, miss,' Cap'n Trucha said to her as she looked over the maps, "Might I, and my crew, have the honor of escorting you and your," he paused and looked at Teddy, "bear to shore?"

"That would be fantastic!" the princess said.

She spent a few more minutes pouring over the maps that they had on the ship until she ran across one with the land she came from. She found and memorized the way to her home and rolled the map up and put it away. Then everyone said their good-byes.

Cap'n Tuna hugged the princess tight and said, "Thank you so very much! Your education came in very handy today! I don't know what we would have done without you, some-one might have gotten hurt!"

"I was more than happy to help and you know, you're right! It really did help, didn't it?!"

Cap'n Trucha escorted Princess Rachel and Teddy onto his ship and barked out orders to his crew. The princess gave the coordinates to the Spanish navigator and they headed toward the shore.

As they drew near, the ship came to a stop. The captain bowed to Princess Rachel and bid her farewell, thanking her for her help and wishing her a safe journey.

She and Teddy climbed down the ladder and waded to the shore, waving good-bye when they reached it. Teddy fell down and kissed the sand. "If I never see a drop of water again," he said, "it will be too soon!"

The princess patted him on the head and they watched the ship sail back out to sea.

Then started walking inland.

Soon the ground was covered with a short, course grass. The princess bent down and examined it. She picked a strand and showed it to Teddy. "This is the type of grass usually found in Africa," she began. "Oh Teddy, we're so far from home!"

"Oooo! I gotta bad feelin' about this!" Teddy mumbled.

They were stopped in their tracks by the roar of a lion and Teddy jumped into Princess Rachel's arms.

"Wha...wha...what was that?!" he asked nervously.

"Lions I'm afraid!" she whispered, looking about.

Five lionesses came out from behind some rocks and circled them slowly. The largest of the small group roared again and yelled, "Intruders! How dare you trespass on our plains!"

A second said, "You are the kind that is our enemy! You are man!"

"And where is the rest of your kind?" a third snarled. "The ones with the guns and the evil hearts that kill us and destroy our land?"

"Let's not wait to find out!" the largest said. "Let's kill them now!"

They crouched for the attack. Teddy scrambled up onto the princess's neck, terrified.

Suddenly a gorilla jumped from a tree between the princess and the lionesses. "Shar-ah! Stop!" she demanded. "You know you cannot kill man! The death of one brings many to our lair and vengeance against our kind! This human must go before King Hehshemah for her fate to be decided!"

Shar-ah roared fiercely. "Very well, Uzuri. We'll take her to the king."

The lionesses surrounded Princess Rachel and Teddy Bearable and escorted them to the King's den.

A crowd of animals gathered as the king watched the princess and the bear closely. He studied them for a long time then spoke. "As ruler I am knowledgeable of all things in the animal kingdom, but I know nothing of this predator called 'man.' Perhaps you can shed some light on what they do."

Shar-ah roared angrily. "Unthinkable Hehshemah! That the king of beasts would look to man for his wisdom!"

"This one is different Shar-ah," he said. "I sense in her a spirit unlike most men. One of quiet, a kindness even. This one is royalty, I can feel it. She is surrounded with peace and love, and I trust her. Am I right your highness?"

The princess smiled and curtsied. "Yes your majesty. I am Princess Rachel from the land of Terrah; this is Teddy Bearable. We are very far from our home and are in the process of heading there."

The king nodded and said, "Humans are invading our land. They are interfering with our hunting."

Uzuri the gorilla stepped next to the king. "They eat the fruit from our trees, stripping them bare."

An elephant, Tembo, swung his trunk angrily in front of his face. "They take members from our herds and make them work!"

The princess shook her head with understanding. "My instructors say it is important to learn and accept the customs of other cultures so that we can share the earth we live on. We're also taught to problem solve. You must look at a situation, decide if it's unchangeable, and if it is, find different ways to deal with what's happening. If you'll take a moment and think, you'll come up with a solution!"

The animals listened closely as she spoke.

"Your Majesty," she continued, "the herds are so large, surely the humans can't be taking that many animals from you! And your lionesses must simply hunt on the days the humans aren't around! You see, we humans have a great fear of you, so you must completely avoid them.

"Uzuri, the fruit on the trees will always grow back! And if you take the seeds and plant them in the ground and water them, a new tree will grow. Then there will be plenty for all to share!

"And Tembo, the elephants from your herd are fed and watered and taken care of, and I have read that when they get too old to work, the human tribes free them to return to you."

King Hehshemah smiled kindly. "I agree with the things you have said, Princess Rachel. I believe it may actually be possible to co-exist here with man. We will do all that is in our power and time will tell. Whoever has taught you, dear child, has taught you very well! When it is your time to take the throne you will no doubt make a great ruler."

The princess smiled and curtsied before the king.

"Your Majesty," Uzuri said, "might I escort Princess Rachel and Teddy Bearable to the end of our land?"

"I would be very pleased if you would," he replied. "Tembo, I would like you to accompany Uzuri and our guests on their journey."

"Yes your Majesty, I would be honored!"

Shar-ah walked to Princess Rachel. "I too would like to go. And I owe you an apology, your highness."

The princess smiled and touched the side of Shar-ah's face gently.

"So you're not going to eat us or tear us to pieces?" Teddy asked nervously.

Everyone laughed.

"Of course not," Shar-ah said.

Teddy sighed and slid down from Princess Rachel's neck.

"Princess Rachel, thank you," King Hehshemah said.

The elephant walked to the princess and knelt down. She climbed onto his back, pulling Teddy up behind her.

Uzuri jumped onto Tembo's trunk and they headed across the pride lands, Shar-ah leading the way.

Quite a few hours had gone by when Uzuri suddenly jumped onto the ground next to Shar-ah.

"This is as far as we can go, your highness," Shar-ah said. "We must leave you to continue on your own."

Princess Rachel slid down the side of Tembo's neck and gave him a big hug. She shook hands with Uzuri and scratched Shar-ah behind her ears.

"Eh, oh! Get me off this big stinky!" Teddy demanded.

Tembo shook hard and dumped the bear onto the ground, head first.

"Oh, that's great!" he grumbled as he stood, brushing himself off. "I'll be picking grass out of my fur for hours!"

Everyone tried not to laugh at the bear, but couldn't keep themselves from it.

Princess Rachel thanked the trio and waved good-bye as she and Teddy set out on foot.

By early evening, Princess Rachel noticed that the grass under their feet grew higher and higher until it had grown as tall as wheat, and off in the distance she could see stalks of corn. Teddy pointed to the farm that stood just past the fields.

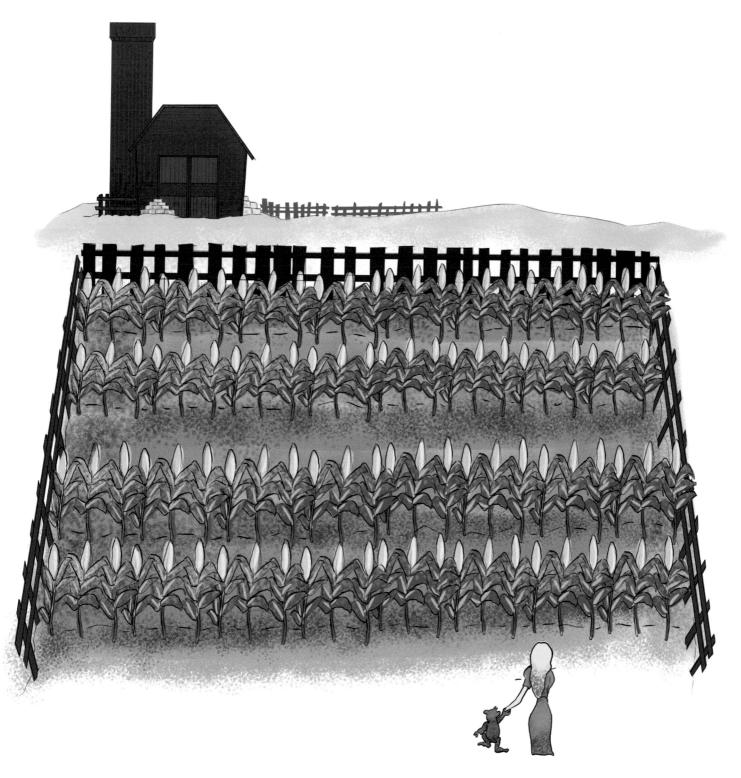

As they approached the barn, the princess noticed how depressed all the animals were.

"What is the matter here?" she asked the pig quietly.

"Oh, it's a sad day!" he replied. "Poor Mrs. Morgan! Her little baby is ill and no one can figure out what to do!"

"Do you think I might be able to take a look at him?" Princess Rachel asked.

The pig shrugged his shoulders and nodded toward the barn door. "They're in there. Elsa, why don't you show them in?"

"Certainly, Snorty." The cow looked up at the princess. "This way, my dear. You see, our farmin' humans are out of town this week and the fella they've got lookin' over us doesn't come till tomorrow morning. Well, I'm afraid it'll be too late for that young'n by then."

"Oh, how awful. I hope I can help!" the princess said.

As the three of them entered the barn, Princess Rachel saw the rest of the animals gathered around the sickly colt. The mother horse pushed some straw up onto her foal.

Teddy said, "Ah, I ah, I think I'll sit this one out! I don't want whatever that kid's got! Thanks, but no thanks!"

The cow snorted at him. "Suit yourself!"

Teddy leaned against a bale of straw just outside the barn and watched them approach the group.

The princess walked up slowly and knelt beside the foal. She noticed his breathing was somewhat labored as if the slightest movement was hurting him. She could see he was very ill. She glanced up at Mrs. Morgan and her heart sank as she saw tears streaming down the horse's face.

"Can you tell me what happened, Ma'am?" Princess Rachel asked her.

"I really have no idea!" she answered. "I went out to the water trough for a drink and a short chat with Casey..." A large draft horse bowed her head. "...and when I came back inside ten minutes later, there was my baby, lying here just as he is now!"

Princess Rachel placed her hand on the colt's neck and felt how unusually sweaty he was. "It's odd how hot he is on this nice cool day. And his breathing is so irregular," she commented.

Teddy looked around the interior of the barn. In a far corner, he noticed a rat hiding in the shadows, laughing and looking very guilty. He crept over and grabbed it tightly by the neck, then carried it to the center of the group and flung it down in disgust. "Hey!" he said, "This thing knows something! I can tell! Just look at it!"

The rat crouched on the ground staring angrily at everyone.

"Napoleon, what do you know about this?!" Casey demanded.

"Nuttin'! So you'ze can all get outta my face!" the rat hissed.

"You're lying!" Elsa accused. "There's a life at stake, you horrible creature!"

"Please Napoleon! If you know anything and can save my son, I need you to tell us!" Mrs. Morgan cried.

Princess Rachel reached down and picked up the rat. "Please help us," she urged.

Napoleon looked at her dreamily. "Well," he said, "I guess I did see that baby eat out of one of those bags over there." He pointed to a stall door that was slightly ajar.

"Of course!" the princess said. "He must have eaten something with poison in it!"

She got up and ran into the stall, throwing the bags of feed around until she saw one that contained rat poison. She brought the bag out into the group and read what was printed on the side. "Hazardous to humans and domestic animals. May be harmful or fatal if swallowed. If eaten, call your doctor or veterinarian. Oral administration of Vitiman K1 are indicated: 10 - 20 mg. See this skull and crossbones?" she asked the group. "That is what humans put on things to show that they are poisonous!"

Snorty stepped close to Napoleon. "Did you tell the colt to eat that poison?"

The rat shifted around nervously.

"Well did you?!" he demanded.

Napoleon snarled. "Yes I did! Those humans are always setting that stuff out for me to eat and I wanted to see if it was O.K.! Why should I eat it if it's going to make me sick like that?!" He pointed to the foal on the ground.

"You dirty rat!" Etta the goose hissed.

"Well I can't read like that beauty there, so what am I supposed to do?"

"You wonder why we're always trying to run you off this ranch," Etta continued, "it's because you're such a mean, selfish, nasty, BAD creature!"

The rat thought for a minute. "All right, all right! How can I help?"

Princess Rachel turned the bag over. "It says here to call a veterinarian, but depending on how much the foal ate, he may just need the medicine. Did you see how much he did eat?"

Napoleon looked around the group. "Not very much."

"O.K., well, then you go into the house, and in the bathroom you may find a bottle of this K1 in the medicine cabinet." She showed Napoleon what the letter and number looked like.

"Now hurry and go!" Elsa said.

Napoleon sneered and rolled his eyes. "Fine, but saving someone goes against everything I was born to do!" he said as he crept away slowly.

Teddy walked up to him. "Hurry up!" he yelled and kicked the rat hard, sending him flying out of the barn.

Napoleon looked back and scurried quickly into the window of the house.

Everyone turned their attention back to the sick colt.

"Get me some water, Teddy," the Princess instructed. "Elsa, find me a blanket and let's get him covered up!"

All the animals hurried to help and waited nervously until Napoleon rushed back into the barn.

"Is this the stuff?" he asked Princess Rachel.

"Better be!" Teddy threatened.

The rat flinched as he handed the small bottle to the princess.

"Yes, Napoleon! Let's see if it works!" she replied. Princess Rachel uncapped the bottle and poured some of the medicine down the colt's throat. "Now we wait!" she said. "Come on everybody, let's leave the colt to his mother."

A few of the animals paced around the barn. Princess Rachel and Teddy went outside with Elsa and Snorty. The others followed.

They waited silently.

After a few minutes, the colt came charging past the group, kicking his heels into the air, followed by Mrs. Morgan. The animals cheered.

"You did it!" Mrs. Morgan sighed. "You did it! Thank you!"

The colt came over to the princess and nudged her happily. All the animals did the same.

Casey shook her head. "Who are you, dear, and where did you come from?" she asked.

"I'm Princess Rachel and this is Teddy Bearable. We're trying to get home to my mother and father. I miss them so!" She knelt down and drew a map in the dirt. "This is my father's kingdom, all the way over here. That is where I live, that's where we are trying to go."

Casey and Mrs. Morgan smiled at each other.

Mrs. Morgan lowered her head and lifted the princess onto her back. "I think I know just how to repay your kindness!" she said.

The cow wrapped her long tongue around Teddy and set him on the horse behind the princess.

Suddenly, Mrs. Morgan sprouted wings. "Casey, keep watch on Sebastian," she said, "I'll be back before morning!"

She flew into the air and all the animals waved and shouted good-bye.

Princess Rachel waved back and looked excitedly ahead.

As they flew higher and further away, the princess could make out her castle in the distance. She smiled happily.

Mrs. Morgan landed some distance from the castle and the princess and Teddy slid to the ground.

"Oh, thank you! Thank you for bringing me home!" the princess gushed.

"Thank you again for saving my son's life!" Mrs. Morgan replied.

Princess Rachel hugged her lovingly and said good-bye.

Then she ran toward the castle, Teddy close on her heels.

The princess started to pull ahead and Teddy grabbed onto the back of her gown, then lost his footing and was dragged behind.

As she neared the draw bridge, she slowed to a walk, out of breath.

"Little help!" Teddy said.

Princess Rachel laughed seeing the poor bear covered with burrs and stickers and grass. She helped him up and brushed him off.

"This is it for me, Princess," he began slowly. "Once we go back inside, I'll just be your ol' stuffed bear again." She shook her head sadly. Kneeling down, she hugged him tight.

"You saved me Teddy," she said, "thank you!" and gave him an extra squeeze.

"Oh, don't get all gushy!" he blushed.

"I love you!" she whispered.

"Well yea, who wouldn't!" He wiped a tear from his eye, then hugged her back tightly. "I love you too!"

The Princess stood and picked up the bear, tucking him under her arm.

She walked over the drawbridge and paused to look into the moat, shaking her head with relief. She let out a long sigh and walked through the castle gates, glad to be home.

The two guards fell all over themselves seeing her there, then came to their senses and bowed.

"Your highness! Princess Rachel!" they cried happily.

The older man put his hand over his heart and said, "We thought…" suddenly he straightened up. "Get the king!!!" he instructed the other.

The second man rushed off yelling for King Jeremiah.

The princess looked down at Teddy Bearable. He stared back at her blankly. "You were a great help, my friend," she whispered softly to him.

Princess Rachel walked slowly toward the interior of the great hall. The king and queen rushed out to her, still in the clothes they had been wearing when she left. Queen Elizabeth held her close and wept. The princess wrapped her arms back around her mother and squeezed her tight. King Jeremiah fell to his knees and clasped his hands together. "Thank you Lord! My daughter is home safe!" he cried.

"Father," Princess Rachel started, "I'm sorry. And you were right."
"I was what?" the king asked.

"Father, I used everything I've been taught by my instructors while I was out there. I needed every bit of education I've gotten to handle the things I came up against. And to find my way home! I'm sorry I doubted your telling me how important my studies were."

King Jeremiah rose to his feet. "My child, you learned a great lesson, I see that. But it would have been a lesson better learned if you had stayed here in the safety of our home and taken my word for it. It would have been far wiser for you to have just believed that I know what I speak of, and it would have been kinder to your mother and me, and all those who care about you, for you not to have put us through what you did by running off that way."

"Yes sir." She held tight to her mother. "As I said before, I'm sorry. I will never do anything so foolish again. I trust that when you think I'm ready, I'll be allowed to wander through the world. And believe me, I'm very happy staying here for as long as that time may be!!!"

And Princess Rachel did just as the good king and queen instructed her, and they all lived happily ever after.

The End